Text copyright © 1982 by Nuove Edizioni Romane s.r.l. Translation copyright © 1991 by Olivia Holmes. Illustrations copyright © 1991 by
Barrett V. Root. Text first published in Italian as *Le grazie di san Tonio* by Nuove Edizioni Romane, Rome. All rights reserved. Tambourine
Books, a division of William Morrow & Co., Inc., 1350 Ave. of the Americas, New York, NY 10019. Printed in U.S.A. Library of
Congress Cataloging in Publication Data   Piumini, Roberto. [Grazie di san Tonio. English] The saint and the circus / by Roberto Piumini;
pictures by Barry Root; translated from the Italian by Olivia Holmes. p. cm. Translation of: Le grazie di san Tonio. Summary: When Filofilo the
circus acrobat loses his balance on the tightrope, an inept saint in Heaven comes to his aid in ways that are more harmful than helpful.
ISBN 0-688-10377-4 (trade)—ISBN 0-688-10378-2 (lib.) [1. Tightrope walking—Fiction. 2. Circus—Fiction. 3. Saints—Fiction.] I.
Root, Barry, ill.   II. Title. PZ7.P6894Sai 1991 [E]—dc20 90-23481 CIP AC 10 9 8 7 6 5 4 3 2 1 First edition

The SAINT

by Roberto Piumini

Translated from the Italian by OLIVIA HOLMES

TAMBOURINE BOOKS · NEW YORK

and the CIRCUS

pictures by Barry Root

Filofilo, the daring acrobat for the Bumbellini Circus, was inching along a tightrope a hundred feet above the ground. He held a long pole in his hands to help keep his balance. Five thousand spectators were following his act with their noses in the air.

Filofilo swayed the pole up and down every now and then, sometimes to get his balance, and sometimes just to give the crowd the thrills they had paid for. Halfway across the rope, he stopped. Holding the pole perfectly still, he nodded his head from side to side to receive the audience's applause. But out of the blue, a sparrow fluttered under the circus tent and landed on one end of the pole.

Filofilo was in trouble. As tiny as the bird was, it upset the acrobat's balance and he started tottering frightfully on the cable. He closed his eyes and cried, "Heaven help me!"

Unfortunately, a certain Saint Tony, who had been made a saint more for his good humor than his good sense, was on duty just then in Heaven's emergency room. It was his turn to stand guard and help anyone on earth who called for heavenly assistance.

Saint Tony figured that if one sparrow made Filofilo lose his balance, then another sparrow would help him get it back. And out of thin air a new sparrow appeared on the other end of the pole. The two balanced each other, and Filofilo stood up straight again. The audience, thinking that this was some sort of wonderful trick, applauded enthusiastically. But then a frightened murmur ran through the crowd.

Saint Tony had sent a pretty girl sparrow to the rescue and the first sparrow had taken a great liking to her. He flew right over to her and started to nudge and stroke her wings, which she didn't mind at all. Now Filofilo was in twice as much trouble as before. Staggering and white with fear, he could only pray, "Heaven help me!"

Saint Tony went into action, thinking, "I have to balance the two sparrows. But if I send two more of them, who knows what complicated friendships and rivalries . . ."

At that very instant a white pigeon flew onto the empty end of the pole. Filofilo straightened up and breathed a sigh of relief. The crowd applauded.

But the sparrows' courtship was over. The lovers flew off on a long honeymoon flight around the tent, holding each other by the tip of the wing.

Now it was the pigeon that was causing trouble. But he didn't know it and stayed where providence had put him. Once more the tightrope walker started his wobbly dance. "Saints in Heaven, make this pigeon go away!" prayed Filofilo, who had decided in desperation to give his heavenly protectors some instructions.

"OK," thought Saint Tony, "what's the best way to get rid of a pigeon?"

Presto! A fat tabby cat appeared on the free end of the pole.

Now it is true that cats are good for making birds go away. But it is even more true that a pole one hundred feet above the ground is no place for a pussycat. Taking no notice of the pigeon, the tabby made a big meowing leap and dug his claws into the most solid thing around—Filofilo's bottom.

The acrobat yelled, the cat yowled, the audience shuddered, and the pigeon bowed his head as if to acknowledge the applause. And Filofilo, all scrunched up with the cat hanging onto him, implored, "Saints! O saints! Send this cat away!"

Saint Tony acted quickly—a big mastiff appeared on the pole, making it dip frighteningly to one side. But the dog only howled. He was much too worried about falling to notice the cat.

The pigeon, who had been sitting calmly at the other end of the pole, thought, "If this dog is the cat's enemy, and the cat is my enemy, then the dog is my friend." His reasoning was not perfect, but you can't expect a pigeon to be smarter than a saint.

The pigeon burst into flight. When the dog started to fall to one side, the pigeon pecked him on that side; when he started to fall to the other, the pigeon pecked him on the other. So the dog kept his balance on the pole, the cat on the acrobat, and the acrobat on the wire, but everything leaned toward the side where the dog was.

The crowd's enthusiasm swelled the circus tent. But Filofilo gasped, "For the love of God, saints, let me get my balance!"

Saint Tony, who had been trying to do just that for quite some time, decided it was useless to send more four-footed animals.

Presto! A big monkey that weighed exactly the same as the dog dangled from the free end of the pole.

But Filofilo, with the tabby's claws upsetting both his balance and his peace of mind, implored once and for all, "Saints in Heaven, help me or else throw me down and put an end to this!"

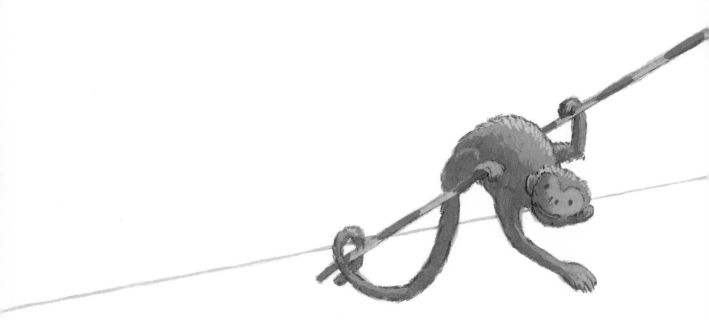

Luckily, Saint Tony's turn was up just then and Saint Ulysses, who was so cunning that he had snuck into Heaven inside a wooden horse, took over. Saint Ulysses decided to perform an extra special rescue. He turned himself into a long blue serpent and wriggled through a hole in the tent as if he had slid down from the moon. Then he knotted himself around Filofilo's feet.

The crowd held its breath, not having expected a blue serpent at that height. Filofilo hadn't really expected one either. He was so terrified that he dropped the pole and toppled off the tightrope.

The dog fell, the cat fell, the monkey fell, and even the pigeon fell, gripping the tail of his friend the dog. But as the animals were all dreamed up by Saint Tony, they disappeared into thin air before touching earth.

And Filofilo, who was real?

Filofilo didn't hit the ground; he hung upside down with his feet caught in the serpent's grip. Then the serpent began to untangle, slowly letting the acrobat down. When Filofilo's hands touched the earth, the long blue snake disappeared in a hundred bursts and sparkles of fireworks. Filofilo stood on his hands for a few moments, then somersaulted to his feet and, not knowing what else to do, bowed and smiled to the crowd.

A roar of applause, cheers, and hurrahs overflowed the tent. Even the monkeys in their cages joined in the clapping. But monkeys imitate what people do without thinking, you know.